DATE DUE

THE RIME
OF THE
ANCIENT MARINER

THE RIME
OF THE
ANCIENT MARINER

BY SAMUEL TAYLOR COLERIDGE
ILLUSTRATED BY ED YOUNG

ATHENEUM · 1992 · NEW YORK

MAXWELL MACMILLAN CANADA
TORONTO

MAXWELL MACMILLAN INTERNATIONAL
NEW YORK OXFORD SINGAPORE SYDNEY

Atheneum
Macmillan Publishing Company
866 Third Avenue
New York, NY 10022

Maxwell Macmillan Canada, Inc.
1200 Eglinton Avenue East
Suite 200
Don Mills, Ontario M3C 3N1

Macmillan Publishing Company is part of the
Maxwell Communication Group of Companies.

First edition

Printed in the United States of America

10 9 8 7 6 5 4 3 2 1

The text of this book is set in Perpetua.
The illustrations are rendered in pastels and charcoal.

Production: Daniel Adlerman.
Art Director: Patrice Fodero.

LIBRARY OF CONGRESS CATALOGING-IN-PUBLICATION DATA

Coleridge, Samuel Taylor, 1772–1834.
    The rime of the ancient mariner/by Samuel Taylor Coleridge; art
by Ed Young.—1st ed.
        p.   cm.
    Summary: In this illustrated edition of the classic poem, a sailor
recounts the terrible fate that befell his ship when he shot down an
albatross.
    ISBN 0–689–31613–5
    [1. English poetry.]   I. Young, Ed, ill.   II. Title
PR4479.A1   1992
821'.7—dc20   90–20403

*To Captain John Lloyd and Priscilla Moulton of
"White Wave," for their constant encouragement
that has both deepened and widened my work.*

— E.Y.

Argument

How a Ship having passed the Line was driven by storms to the cold Country towards the South Pole; and how from thence she made her course to the tropical Latitude of the Great Pacific Ocean; and of the strange things that befell: and in what manner the Ancyent Marinere came back to his own Country.

PART 1

An ancient Mariner
meeteth three Gallants
bidden to a
wedding-feast, and
detaineth one.

It is an ancient Mariner,
And he stoppeth one of three.
"By thy long gray beard and glittering eye,
Now wherefore stopp'st thou me?

"The Bridegroom's doors are opened wide,
And I am next of kin,
The guests are met, the feast is set:
May'st hear the merry din."

He holds him with his skinny hand;
"There was a ship," quoth he.
"Hold off! unhand me, gray-beard loon!"
Eftsoons his hand dropt he.

The Wedding-Guest is
spellbound by the eye of
the old seafaring man
and constrained to hear
his tale.

He holds him with his glittering eye—
The Wedding-Guest stood still,
And listens like a three years' child.
The Mariner hath his will.

The Wedding-Guest sat on a stone:
He cannot choose but hear;
And thus spake on that ancient man,
The bright-eyed Mariner.

"The ship was cheered, the harbor cleared,
Merrily did we drop
Below the kirk, below the hill,
Below the light-house top.

The Mariner tells how
the ship sailed
southward with a good
wind and fair weather,
till it reached the Line.

"The sun came up upon the left,
Out of the sea came he!
And he shone bright, and on the right
Went down into the sea.

"Higher and higher every day,
Till over the mast at noon—"
The Wedding-Guest here beat his breast,
For he heard the loud bassoon.

The bride hath paced into the hall,
Red as a rose is she;
Nodding their heads before her goes
The merry minstrelsy.

*The Wedding-Guest
heareth the bridal music;
but the Mariner
continueth his tale.*

The Wedding - Guest he beat his breast,
Yet he cannot choose but hear;
And thus spake on that ancient man,
The bright-eyed Mariner.

"And now the Storm-blast came, and he
Was tyrannous and strong:
He struck with his o'ertaking wings,
And chased us south along.

*The ship driven by a
storm toward the south
pole.*

"With sloping masts and dipping prow,
As who pursued with yell and blow
Still treads the shadow of his foe,
And forward bends his head,
The ship drove fast, loud roared the blast,
And southward aye we fled.

"And now there came both mist and snow,
And it grew wondrous cold:
And ice, mast-high, came floating by,
As green as emerald.

"And through the drifts the snowy clifts
Did send a dismal sheen:
Nor shapes of men nor beasts we ken—
The ice was all between.

"The ice was here - the ice was there,
The ice was all around:
It cracked and growled, and roared and howled,
Like noises in a swound!

"At length did cross an Albatross,
Thorough the fog it came;
As if it had been a Christian soul,
We hailed it in God's name.

"It ate the food it ne'er had eat,
And round and round it flew.
The ice did split with a thunder-fit;
The helmsman steered us through!

"And a good south wind sprung up behind;
The Albatross did follow,
And every day, for food or play,
Came to the mariners' hollo!

"In mist or cloud, on mast or shroud,
It perched for vespers nine;
Whiles all the night, through fog-smoke white,
Glimmered the white moon-shine."

And lo! the Albatross proveth a bird of good omen, and followeth the ship as it returned northward through fog and floating ice.

"God save thee, ancient Mariner!
From the fiends, that plague thee thus!–
Why look'st thou so?"–"With my cross-bow
I shot the Albatross!"

PART II

"The Sun now rose upon the right:
Out of the sea came he,
Still hid in mist, and on the left
Went down into the sea.

"And the good south wind still blew behind,
But no sweet bird did follow,
Nor any day for food or play
Came to the mariners' hollo!

His shipmates cry out against the ancient Mariner, for killing the bird of good luck.

"And I had done a hellish thing,
And it would work 'em woe:
For all averred, I had killed the bird
That made the breeze to blow.
Ah, wretch! said they, the bird to slay,
That made the breeze to blow!

But when the fog cleared off they justify the same, and thus make themselves accomplices in the crime.

"Nor dim nor red, like God's own head,
The glorious Sun uprist:
Then all averred, I had killed the bird
That brought the fog and mist.
'Twas right, said they, such birds to slay,
That bring the fog and mist.

The fair breeze continues; the ship enters the Pacific Ocean, and sails northward, even till it reaches the Line.

"The fair breeze blew, the white foam flew,
The furrow followed free;
We were the first that ever burst
Into that silent sea.

The ship hath been suddenly becalmed.

"Down dropt the breeze, the sails dropt down,
'Twas sad as sad could be;
And we did speak only to break
The silence of the sea!

"All in a hot and copper sky,
The bloody Sun, at noon,
Right up above the mast did stand,
No bigger than the Moon.

"Day after day, day after day,
We stuck, nor breath nor motion;
As idle as a painted ship
Upon a painted ocean.

*And the Albatross begins
to be avenged.*

"Water, water, everywhere,
And all the boards did shrink;
Water, water, everywhere,
Nor any drop to drink.

"The very deep did rot: O Christ!
That ever this should be!
Yea, slimy things did crawl with legs
Upon the slimy sea.

"About, about, in reel and rout
The death-fires danced at night;
The water, like a witch's oils,
Burnt green, and blue and white.

*A Spirit had followed
them; one of the invisible
inhabitants of this
planet, neither departed
souls nor angels;
concerning whom the
learned Jew, Josephus,
and the Platonic
Constantinopolitan,
Michael Psellus, may be
consulted. They are very
numerous, and there is
no climate or element
without one or more.*

"And some in dreams assured were
Of the spirit that plagued us so,
Nine fathom deep he had followed us
From the land of mist and snow.

"And every tongue, through utter drought,
Was withered at the root;
We could not speak, no more than if
We had been choked with soot.

The shipmates, in their
sore distress, would fain
throw the whole guilt on
the ancient Mariner: in
sign whereof they hang
the dead sea-bird round
his neck.

"Ah! well-a-day! what evil looks
Had I from old and young!
Instead of the cross, the Albatross
About my neck was hung.

PART III

"There passed a weary time. Each throat
Was parched, and glazed each eye.
A weary time! a weary time!
How glazed each weary eye,
When looking westward, I beheld
A something in the sky.

"At first it seemed a little speck,
And then it seemed a mist;
It moved and moved, and took at last
A certain shape, I wist.

"A speck, a mist, a shape, I wist!
And still it neared and neared:
As if it dodged a water-sprite,
It plunged and tacked and veered.

"With throats unslaked, with black lips baked,
We could nor laugh nor wail;
Through utter drought all dumb we stood!
I bit my arm, I sucked the blood,
And cried, A sail! a sail!

"With throats unslaked, with black lips baked,
Agape they heard me call:
Gramercy! they for joy did grin,
And all at once their breath drew in,
As they were drinking all.

A flash of joy;

"See! see! (I cried) she tacks no more!
Hither to work us weal—
Without a breeze, without a tide,
She steadies with upright keel!

And horror follows. For can it be a ship that comes onward without wind or tide?

"The western wave was all aflame,
The day was well nigh done!
Almost upon the western wave
Rested the broad bright Sun;
When that strange shape drove suddenly
Betwixt us and the Sun.

"And straight the Sun was flecked with bars,
(Heaven's Mother send us grace!)
As if through a dungeon-grate he peered
With broad and burning face.

It seemeth him but the skeleton of a ship.

"Alas! (thought I, and my heart beat loud)
How fast she nears and nears!
Are those her sails that glance in the Sun,
Like restless gossameres?

"Are those her ribs through which the Sun
Did peer, as through a grate?

And its ribs are seen as bars on the face of the setting Sun.

*The Specter-Woman and
her Deathmate, and no
other on board the
skeleton-ship.*

And is that Woman all her crew?
Is that a Death? and are there two?
Is Death that woman's mate?

Like vessel, like crew!

"Her lips were red, her looks were free,
Her locks were yellow as gold:
Her skin was as white as leprosy,
The Night-mare Life-in-Death was she,
Who thicks man's blood with cold.

*Death and
Life-in-Death have diced
for the ship's crew, and
she (the latter) winneth
the ancient Mariner.*

"The naked hulk alongside came,
And the twain were casting dice;
'The game is done! I've won! I've won!'
Quoth she, and whistles thrice.

*No twilight within the
courts of the Sun.*

"The Sun's rim dips; the stars rush out:
At one stride comes the dark;
With far-heard whisper, o'er the sea,
Off shot the specter-bark.

*At the rising of the
Moon,*

"We listened and looked sideways up!
Fear at my heart, as at a cup,
My life-blood seemed to sip!
The stars were dim, and thick the night,
The steersman's face by his lamp gleamed white;
From the sails the dew did drip—
Till clomb above the eastern bar
The hornéd Moon, with one bright star
Within the nether tip.

One after another,

"One after one, by the star-dogged Moon,
Too quick for groan or sigh,
Each turned his face with a ghastly pang,
And cursed me with his eye.

"Four times fifty living men,
(And I heard nor sigh nor groan)
With heavy thump, a lifeless lump
They dropt down one by one.

"The souls did from their bodies fly—
They fled to bliss or woe!
And every soul, it passed me by
Like the whizz of my cross-bow!"

*His shipmates drop
down dead.*

*But Life-in-Death
begins her work on the
ancient Mariner.*

PART IV

The Wedding-Guest
feareth that a Spirit is
talking to him;

"I fear thee, ancient Mariner!
I fear thy skinny hand!
And thou art long, and lank, and brown,
As is the ribbed sea-sand.

"I fear thee and thy glittering eye,
And thy skinny hand, so brown."–

But the
ancient Mariner
assureth him of his
bodily life, and
proceedeth to relate his
horrible penance.

"Fear not, fear not, thou Wedding-Guest!
This body dropt not down.

"Alone, alone, all, all alone,
Alone on a wide, wide sea!
And never a saint took pity on
My soul in agony.

"The many men, so beautiful!
And they all dead did lie:
And a thousand thousand slimy things
Lived on; and so did I.

And envieth that they
should live, and so many
lie dead.

"I looked upon the rotting sea,
And drew my eyes away;
I looked upon the rotting deck,
and there the dead men lay.

"I looked to heaven, and tried to pray;
But or ever a prayer had gusht,
A wicked whisper came, and made
My heart as dry as dust.

"I closed my lids, and kept them close,
And the balls like pulses beat;
For the sky and the sea, and the sea and the sky
Lay like a load on my weary eye,
And the dead were at my feet.

"The cold sweat melted from their limbs,
Nor rot nor reek did they:
The look with which they looked on me
Had never passed away.

*But the curse liveth for
him in the eye of the
dead men.*

"An orphan's curse would drag to hell
A spirit from on high;
But oh! more horrible than that
Is a curse in a dead man's eye!
Seven days, seven nights, I saw that curse,
And yet I could not die.

"The moving Moon went up the sky,
And nowhere did abide:
Softly she was going up,
And a star or two beside—

*In his loneliness and
fixedness he yearneth
towards the journeying
Moon, and the stars that
still sojourn, yet still
move onward; and
everywhere the blue sky
belongs to them, and is
their appointed rest, and
their native country and
their own natural
homes, which they enter
unannounced, as lords
that are certainly
expected, and yet there is
a silent joy at their
arrival.*

"Her beams bemocked the sultry main,
Like April hoar-frost spread;
But where the ship's huge shadow lay,
The charmèd water burnt alway
A still and awful red.

"Beyond the shadow of the ship,
I watched the water-snakes:
They moved in tracks of shining white
And when they reared, the elfish light
Fell off in hoary flakes.

*By the light of the Moon
he beholdeth God's
creatures of the great
calm.*

"Within the shadow of the ship
I watched their rich attire:
Blue, glossy green, and velvet black,
They coiled and swam; and every track
Was a flash of golden fire.

"O happy living things! no tongue
Their beauty might declare:
A spring of love gushed from my heart,
And I blessed them unaware;
Sure my kind saint took pity on me,
And I blessed them unaware.

"The selfsame moment I could pray;
And from my neck so free
The Albatross fell off, and sank
Like lead into the sea."

Their beauty and their happiness.

He blesseth them in his heart.

The spell begins to break.

PART V

"Oh sleep! it is a gentle thing,
Beloved from pole to pole!
To Mary Queen the praise be given!
She sent the gentle sleep from Heaven,
That slid into my soul.

"The silly buckets on the deck,
That had so long remained,
I dreamt that they were filled with dew;
And when I awoke, it rained.

"My lips were wet, my throat was cold,
My garments all were dank;
Sure I had drunken in my dreams,
And still my body drank.

"I moved, and could not feel my limbs:
I was so light—almost
I thought that I had died in sleep,
And was a blessed ghost.

"And soon I heard a roaring wind
It did not come anear;
But with its sound it shook the sails,
That were so thin and sere.

"The upper air burst into life!
And a hundred fire-flags sheen,
To and fro they were hurried about!
And to and fro, and in and out,
The wan stars danced between.

"And the coming wind did roar more loud,
And the sails did sigh like sedge.
And the rain poured down from one black cloud;
The Moon was at its edge.

"The thick black cloud was cleft, and still
The Moon was at its side:
Like waters shot from some high crag,
The lightning fell with never a jag,
A river steep and wide.

"The loud wind never reached the ship,
Yet now the ship moved on!
Beneath the lightning and the Moon
The dead men gave a groan.

"They groaned, they stirred, they all uprose,
Nor spake, nor moved their eyes;
It had been strange, even in a dream,
To have seen those dead men rise.

"The helmsman steered, the ship moved on;
Yet never a breeze up blew;
The mariners all 'gan work the ropes,
Where they were wont to do;
They raised their limbs like lifeless tools—
We were a ghastly crew.

"The body of my brother's son
Stood by me, knee to knee:
The body and I pulled at one rope,
But he said nought to me."

The bodies of the ship's crew are inspired, and the ship moves on;

But not by the souls of
the men, nor by demons
of earth or middle air,
but by a blessed troop of
angelic spirits, sent
down by the invocation
of the guardian saint.

"I fear thee, ancient Mariner!"
"Be calm, thou Wedding-Guest!
'Twas not those souls that fled in pain,
Which to their corses came again,
But a troop of spirits blest:

"For when it dawned—they dropped their arms,
And clustered round the mast;
Sweet sounds rose slowly through their mouths,
And from their bodies passed.

"Around, around, flew each sweet sound,
Then darted to the Sun;
Slowly the sounds came back again,
Now mixed, now one by one.

"Sometimes a-dropping from the sky
I heard the skylark sing;
Sometimes all little birds that are,
How they seemed to fill the sea and air
With their sweet jargoning!

"And now 'twas like all instruments,
Now like a lonely flute;
And now it is an angel's song,
That makes the heavens be mute.

"It ceased; yet still the sails made on
A pleasant noise till noon,
A noise like of a hidden brook
In the leafy month of June,
That to the sleeping woods all night
Singeth a quiet tune.

"Till noon we quietly sailed on,
Yet never a breeze did breathe:
Slowly and smoothly went the ship,
Moved onward from beneath.

*The lonesome Spirit from
the south pole carries on
the ship as far as the
Line, in obedience to the
angelic troop, but still
requireth vengeance.*

"Under the keel nine fathom deep,
From the land of mist and snow,
The Spirit slid: and it was he
That made the ship to go.
The sails at noon left off their tune,
And the ship stood still also.

"The Sun, right up above the mast,
Had fixed her to the ocean:
But in a minute she 'gan stir,
With a short uneasy motion—
Backwards and forwards half her length
With a short uneasy motion.

"Then like a pawing horse let go,
She made a sudden bound:
It flung the blood into my head,
And I fell down in a swound.

*The Polar Spirit's fellow
demons, the invisible
inhabitants of the
element, take part in his
wrong; and two of them
relate, one to the other
that penance long and
heavy for the ancient
Mariner hath been
accorded to the Polar
Spirit, who returneth
southward.*

"How long in that same fit I lay,
I have not to declare;
But ere my living life returned,
I heard, and in my soul discerned,
Two voices in the air.

"'Is it he?' quoth one, 'Is this the man?
By Him who died on cross,
With his cruel bow he laid full low
The harmless Albatross.

"'The Spirit who bideth by himself
In the land of mist and snow,
He loved the bird that loved the man
Who shot him with his bow.'

"The other was a softer voice,
As soft as honey-dew:
Quoth he, 'The man hath penance done,
And penance more will do.'"

PART VI

FIRST VOICE
" 'But tell me, tell me! speak again,
Thy soft response renewing—
What makes that ship drive on so fast?
What is the ocean doing?'

SECOND VOICE
" 'Still as a slave before his lord,
The ocean hath no blast;
His great bright eye most silently
Up to the Moon is cast—

" 'If he may know which way to go;
For she guides him smooth or grim.
See, brother, see! how graciously
She looketh down on him.'

FIRST VOICE
" 'But why drives on that ship so fast,
Without or wave or wind?'

SECOND VOICE
" 'The air is cut away before,
And closes from behind.'
" 'Fly, brother, fly! more high, more high!
Or we shall be belated:
For slow and slow that ship will go,
When the Mariner's trance is abated.'

The Mariner hath been cast into a trance; for the angelic power causeth the vessel to drive northward faster than human life could endure.

"I woke, and we were sailing on
As in a gentle weather:
'Twas night, calm night, the moon was high;
The dead men stood together.

"All stood together on the deck,
For a charnel-dungeon fitter:
All fixed on me their stony eyes,
That in the Moon did glitter.

"The pang, the curse, with which they died,
Had never passed away:
I could not draw my eyes from theirs,
Nor turn them up to pray.

"And now this spell was snapt: once more
I viewed the ocean green,
And looked far forth, yet little saw
Of what had else been seen—

"Like one, that on a lonesome road
Doth walk in fear and dread,
And having once turned round, walks on,
And turns no more his head.
Because he knows, a frightful fiend
Doth close behind him tread.

"But soon there breathed a wind on me,
Nor sound nor motion made:
Its path was not upon the sea,
In ripple or in shade.

The supernatural motion is retarded; the Mariner awakes, and his penance begins anew.

The curse is finally expiated.

"It raised my hair, it fanned my cheek
Like a meadow-gale of spring—
It mingled strangely with my fears,
Yet it felt like a welcoming.

"Swiftly, swiftly flew the ship,
Yet she sailed softly too:
Sweetly, sweetly blew the breeze—
On me alone it blew.

And the ancient Mariner beholdeth his native country.

"Oh! dream of joy! is this indeed
The light-house top I see?
Is this the hill? is this the kirk?
Is this mine own countree?

"We drifted o'er the harbor-bar,
And I with sobs did pray—
O let me be awake, my God!
Or let me sleep alway.

"The harbor-bay was clear as glass,
So smoothly it was strewn!
And on the bay the moonlight lay,
And the shadow of the Moon.

"The rock shone bright, the kirk no less,
That stands above the rock:
The moonlight steeped in silentness
The steady weathercock.

"And the bay was white with silent light
Till, rising from the same,
Full many shapes, that shadows were,
In crimson colors came.

The angelic spirits leave the dead bodies,

"A little distance from the prow
Those crimson shadows were:
I turned my eyes upon the deck—
Oh, Christ! what saw I there!

"Each corse lay flat, lifeless and flat,
And, by the holy rood!
A man all light, a seraph-man,
On every corse there stood.

And appear in their own forms of light.

"This seraph-band, each waved his hand:
It was a heavenly sight!
They stood as signals to the land,
Each one a lovely light;

"This seraph-band, each waved his hand,
No voice did they impart—
No voice; but oh! the silence sank
Like music on my heart.

"But soon I heard the dash of oars,
I heard the Pilot's cheer;
My head was turned perforce away,
And I saw a boat appear.

"The Pilot and the Pilot's boy,
I heard them coming fast:
Dear Lord in Heaven! it was a joy
The dead men could not blast.

"I saw a third—I heard his voice:
It is the Hermit good!
He singeth loud his godly hymns
That he makes in the wood.
He'll shrieve my soul, he'll wash away
The Albatross's blood."

PART VII

"This Hermit good lives in that wood
Which slopes down to the sea.
How loudly his sweet voice he rears!
He loves to talk with marineres
That come from a far countree.

"He kneels at morn, and noon, and eve—
He hath a cushion plump:
It is the moss that wholly hides
The rotted old oak-stump.

"The skiff-boat neared: I heard them talk,
'Why, this is strange, I trow!
Where are those lights so many and fair,
That signal made but now?'

"'Strange, by my faith!' the Hermit said—
'And they answered not our cheer!
The planks looked warped! and see those sails,
How thin they are and sere!
I never saw aught like to them,
Unless perchance it were

"'Brown skeletons of leaves that lag
My forest-brook along.
When the ivy-tod is heavy with snow,
And the owlet whoops to the wolf below,
That eats the she-wolf's young.'

"'Dear Lord! it hath a fiendish look—
(The Pilot made reply)
I am a-feared'—'Push on, push on!'
Said the Hermit cheerily.

"The boat came closer to the ship,
But I nor spake nor stirred.
The boat came close beneath the ship,
And straight a sound was heard.

"Under the water it rumbled on,
Still louder and more dread:
It reached the ship, it split the bay;
The ship went down like lead.

The ship suddenly sinketh.

"Stunned by that loud and dreadful sound,
Which sky and ocean smote,
Like one that hath been seven days drowned
My body lay afloat;
But swift as dreams, myself I found
Within the Pilot's boat.

The ancient Mariner is saved in the Pilot's boat.

"Upon the whirl, where sank the ship,
The boat spun round and round;
And all was still, save that the hill
Was telling of the sound.

"I moved my lips—the Pilot shrieked
And fell down in a fit;
The holy Hermit raised his eyes,
And prayed where he did sit.

"I took the oars: the Pilot's boy,
Who now doth crazy go,
Laughed loud and long, and all the while
His eyes went to and fro.
'Ha! ha!' quoth he, 'full plain I see,
The Devil knows how to row.'

"And now, all in my own countree,
I stood on the firm land!
The Hermit stepped forth from the boat,
And scarcely he could stand.

"'O shrieve me, shrieve me, holy man!"
The Hermit crossed his brow.
'Say quick,' quoth he, 'I bid thee say—
What manner of man art thou?'

"Forthwith this frame of mine was wrenched
With a woful agony,
Which forced me to begin my tale;
And then it left me free.

*The ancient Mariner
earnestly entreateth the
Hermit to shrieve him,
and the penance of life
falls on him.*

"Since then, at an uncertain hour,
That agony returns;
And till my ghastly tale is told,
This heart within me burns.

"I pass, like night, from land to land
I have strange power of speech.
That moment that his face I see,
I know the man that must hear me:
To him my tale I teach.

"What loud uproar bursts from that door!
The wedding-guests are there:
But in the garden-bower the bride
And bride-maids singing are:
And hark the little vesper bell,
Which biddeth me to prayer!

"O Wedding-Guest! this soul hath been
Alone on a wide, wide sea:
So lonely 'twas, that God himself
Scarce seeméd there to be.

"O sweeter than the marriage-feast,
'Tis sweeter far to me,
To walk together to the kirk
With a goodly company!—

And ever and anon throughout his future life an agony constraineth him to travel from land to land.

"To walk together to the kirk,
And all together pray,
While each to his great Father bends,
Old men, and babes, and loving friends,
And youths and maidens gay!

"Farewell, farewell! but this I tell
To thee, thou Wedding-Guest!
He prayeth well, who loveth well
Both man and bird and beast.

And to teach by his own example love and reverence to all things that God made and loveth.

"He prayeth best, who loveth best
All things both great and small;
For the dear God who loveth us,
He made and loveth all."

The Mariner, whose eye is bright,
Whose beard with age is hoar,
Is gone: and now the Wedding-Guest
Turned from the bridegroom's door.

He went like one that hath been stunned,
And is of sense forlorn:
A sadder and a wiser man,
He rose the morrow morn.

(1797-1798; 1798)